The Butter House

The Butter House
by Sarah Gerard

Published in the United States of America
Conium Press
http://www.coniumreview.com

Limited edition hardcover
978-1-942387-20-6

Cover Artwork: Victoria Novak
Book Editing, Design, and Layout: James R. Gapinski

The Butter House

Sarah Gerard

Conium Press
Portland, OR

For Patrick (and Juan, Franny, and Roslyn)

The Butter House

They name it when they arrive, on the cusp of the two brightest seasons, to see the house smiling in the afternoon. Creamy yellow, one story, with a ruddy roof. A Craftsman on a quiet brick street of historic bungalows, their wide shady porches like skirts decked in plumeria. With working A/C, they were assured. It's still months until hurricane season. They're looking fondly toward no-white Christmas.

The girlfriend peeks over the wooden fence into the backyard, seldom mowed. Wildflowers. Prime for a garden. In need of love.

Rusty jalousie windows with screens falling out, bugs worming in. Still, the place has real charm. Not like her hovel of a Brooklyn studio, first floor, down the block from a hospital, no trees, crawling with mice and roaches. She shakes the thought of it.

Keys in the mailbox, the boyfriend's uncle had said. The boyfriend lets them in. Pastel-painted accent walls, hardwood floors. Lots of light. The house is furnished but undecorated, the cabinets empty, the beds unmade.

Turning back toward the car, they encounter a small grey cat seated on the front step. Moony green eyes in a tiny face. Waifish. Waiting. A high-pitched squeak and a tennis ball head in the girlfriend's outstretched hand.

The boyfriend notes one tip of her ear is missing, cut clean across, the work of a local Trap-Neuter-Release program. Hinting: this supposed kitten is older than her size suggests, and can take care of herself, and doesn't need to be adopted into their care. Her small size isn't due to youth but rather to many hardscrabble years and clever adaptations. One of which, likely, is emotional manipulation. Being cute on purpose.

Still, the girlfriend feels a twinge. Possibly fueled by her exuberance for the two of them to be living together, finally, and in such idyllic surrounds—warm, florid, unclouded. And to be merging their costs of living—financial, physical, mental, and emotional. Finally, after saving, starving, striving, they have escaped the big, smelly, loud, expensive, dangerous, filthy city together, to make a home, and contemplate a future, and perhaps even distantly, a family.

They proceed to the car, where the boyfriend retrieves their suitcases. She lifts two mesh carriers from the backseat; they struggle and mew. She makes a beeline for the bedrooms and deposits them each in one, closing the doors.

Later, she sets a plate of kibble outside.

They left at the end of their joint school year (same university, different schools).

For him, this year will be spent observing and documenting the numbers, habits, habitats, movements, and behaviors, both feeding and mating, and linked resilience, of the white ibis, for the state's wildlife agency.

For her, this is a postgraduate year of breathing. Studying. Reassessing. Regrouping. She has completed her psychology internship, but with no immediate job offers, and no license to practice in this new state, she has discovered within herself a shocking lack of disappointment. In fact, relief. Plus confusion. Plus fear.

She finds unpacking to be a useful outlet. She flits nervously in and out of the bungalow's rooms like a nesting bird, emptying boxes and depositing photos on walls, books on shelves, and linens and toiletries in cabinets. Most importantly, she stacks beside their bed the wooden cigar boxes containing her sentimental concert stubs and movie tickets and smooth stones saved on river vacations. On top, she places the one containing dried petals from every flower the boyfriend has ever given her.

She transfers her weight from a kneeling position to a sitting one and spends a moment with a love letter lifted from one of the treasure troves. The boyfriend had left it in her department mailbox, after what she had not realized was a date in the university commons. His handwriting is neat and miniature. Their seat near the window had illuminated her heterochromia iridis, the letter informed her. Does she know how rare she is? Only 0.0006 percent of the country's population has different-colored eyes.

Two triangles appear from beneath the bed. She

runs her hand over her Buddy's smooth back, soft and cool, as he places a tentative paw on her thigh. She tents her knees and lifts him into the crux of her legs and body, trapping him between arms. One hand holds the extended letter while the other gently insists he relax into a purring bundle against her chest. He kneads her skin through her T-shirt as she continues reading. She massages the back of his neck while she finishes the letter, sighs happily, and returns it to its home. She gazes down into this creature still warm against her body, seeing his pupils expand at the precise moment she feels a surge of maternal affection. She truly and sincerely feels she would die for this animal. Kill, even.

She kisses his pink nose.

A distant sound sends him bounding.

Across the hall from their new bedroom, the shared office is painted a pale seafoam and is divided in half by a woven folding screen. Her gaze falls on the boyfriend's simple, glass-top desk, and then beyond the window, descends into a tangle of palm fronds. Standing with an armful of files, she is surprised to realize she doesn't hear traffic, or an ambulance, or a jackhammer, or slamming doors, or echoing voices of neighbors between buildings. She hears nothing. She listens to the nothing. In this silence, smaller sounds emerge, bubbles rising to the surface of still water. A mourning dove coos. A windchime. A bright yellow grasshopper pedals its back legs. Someone's distant whistle reaches her on the breeze. She exhales.

She collapses a stack of cardboard husks and binds them with twine, to carry them to the alley. On her way, she scans the yard for any sign of a grey pelt, *pspspsps*…

For their two cats, cohabitation is an adjustment. Having, like they, never lived together. Knowing nothing of each other, not really, until now. Despite the girlfriend's attempts, after reading up on helpful methods, to acclimate them to the idea of each other in advance. She made a point to talk about the boyfriend's Old Lady in her Little Guy's presence, and vice versa. And to introduce her boyfriend's Old Lady to her future step-sibling's scent via shared toys passed between apartments, after the careful smooshing of them against salivary and anal glands.

The elderly one, the boyfriend's, is an all-black, longhair matron. Yellow eyes. Stage two kidney disease and lymphoma, occasionally necessitating rushing her to the emergency vet for colonics. A docile old dame. A sleek swan whom the girlfriend, attempting pre-adoptive kinship with this awesome creature, has nicknamed: Princess Puma, Puma Love, Shadow Cat, Midnight Cat, Talking Cat, Cat Moonchild, Lady of the Night, and She's So Mysterious / She's So Elegant.

On occasions when the boyfriend was out of town and she was cat-sitter, she would spend the night at his nearby apartment to keep Puma Love company. Would arrive for their sleepovers ready with rotisserie chicken, witnessing and laughing at herself for this elaborate show of effort. She had never had pets growing up, not even fish, having been raised by the kind of parents who make a person want to study psychology. She'd also never, until she fell in love with this man who requests pictures of his cat when he's away for the night, considered parenthood for herself.

Princess Puma couldn't be more different from her own Little Buddy, though. Her Tiny One. Cutie Cat. Cotton Ball Feet. Class Clown. A grey tabby runt belonging to both she and the boyfriend—historically though not practically, as it must be noted that the Son Cat is more bonded with the girlfriend than with the boyfriend, having, until now, only lived with her.

That is, since his rescue. From the hard-knock life of the urban streets.

More on which:

One night late, tipsy, returning from a date. Early in their courting. The cold penetrating their fall jackets, coming through the weave sharply, a late September snap.

They shivered together, huddled, horny and clinging. They made the panicked choice to walk back to her place, which was minutes closer to the train than his was, just as the rain started—first a drizzle, then a freezing sleet.

It was the second week in a row they'd seen That Little Guy. As they later told the story, he was terrified, clearly starving, in teeny tiny white socks, alone, scampering through grease puddles and freezing. Probably subsisting on bugs and trash. Darting from between parked cars, desperate, right up to the new lovers. Huge hungry green eyes hoping, searching them: Is it you? Will you save me?

His tail curled around her ankles. Street-Cat-Tar-in-His-Paws, she called him, noting the black spot beneath one foot (later discovered to be his only non-pink bean).

She couldn't believe he hadn't frozen that bitter night.

He followed them or she coaxed him partway down the block. Then stopped to carry him, unable to see him suffering any longer. He was quivering as she zipped him into her coat. He inhaled two cans of tuna back in her kitchen, licking the sides, then she bathed him and tucked him into bed.

The next day, she bought him scratch pads and a window perch. Later they'd learn he'd been spayed, not neutered. They don't talk about who might have spayed him. Or why he was so healthy, according to the vet. Or so socialized. They don't talk about the flyer the boyfriend saw a month later, outside a bodega.

They put two crates on the floor, doors facing, latched. Hissing. Scrabbling, anger, confusion . . .

Growling. Calm.

Soft hissing. Louder.

Hissing, growling . . .

Grumbling . . .

Growling . . .

Fury!

Refusal!!!

REFUSAL!!!!!

A flurry of screeching and claws against bars.

Fangs!

A swoop to adjacent rooms.

The closing of doors.

They'll try again later.

For days the new siblings, or forced roommates, are given turns to roam The Butter House. They stake claims to their territories, sliding along the new blue velvet couch, scritch-scratching its arms, which had been the most difficult part of its hours-long assembly. Clawing their vintage pink wingback chairs, which had cost real money to ship, as the girlfriend refused to abandon them on the sidewalk in Brooklyn. Curling up for peaceful hours-long naps in a fabric box used to store socks, only for the girlfriend to discover later the little gifts left behind in it.

Smelling each other beneath the closed bedroom door, shredding the boyfriend's inherited Iranian rug when either one grows restless in their confinement. They beg to be released, especially the boy cat. He's so demanding. And naughty. The girlfriend bends to play with his paws beneath the door from time to time, to let him know he isn't forgotten. She flicks treats underneath it, to reward him for being patient.

However, the soul wants freedom, and will insist on it. One night, carrying water back to bed, the girlfriend forgets herself. She cracks the bedroom door, and Street Cat darts between her ankles into the hallway. Stumbling in the darkness, she set her glass on a windowsill before dropping it. Sucks in air through her teeth, disturbing the mattress, grasping at stubbed toes.

The boyfriend sits up beside her. Applies ointment to a bleeding toenail. Bandages the wound.

It will take time for everyone to acclimate, they agree.

They lie down again.

The girlfriend thinks of their stupid argument. It had ruined the otherwise fine day. Had escalated into a metaphor for their relationship. Her sloppiness; his micromanagement. It had been her understanding that the existence of a dishwasher negated the necessity for washing by hand. Guess not.

He wraps his arm around her waist. Sighs into her hair. She closes her eyes and laces her fingers through his. It will take time, she thinks.

She is nearly asleep again when she hears Queen Fur Purr alight upon the windowsill and tap-tap softly above their heads. Then the tinkle of drinking. She cracks an eyelid to see her lapping at the girlfriend's glass, silhouetted against the moon.

The boyfriend orders a baby gate. They install it between the living room and the hallway leading to the bedrooms and assign each cat a zone.

They leap over the gate to chase each other. They fight and win, or lose, and mope by hiding in the closet. The Puma poops behind the couch in protest and tells no one, they just smell it while they're reading. Someone drags their ass across the boyfriend's grandmother's rug.

Then Buff Boi has to go and prove he's a big guy by attacking a damn geriatric lady in her litterbox.

The hallway connecting the kitchen and the bedrooms becomes a highly contested territory where zoom-and-bops might happen to anyone at any time.

For weeks upon weeks, they suffer coffee-table-centric upstairs/downstairs batting wars and under-the-bed battles that disrupt otherwise peaceful and romantic movie nights, cast onto the bedroom room wall with a projector inherited from the psychology department's grant for new equipment, and the subsequent clearing-out and inheriting of old. One useful tool she took away from those years.

Hearing the boyfriend comment on how Cher's very Italian family argues so loudly yet lovingly in Moonstruck, she recalls her family counseling classes. As in her own family, and as he knows, the presence of conflict does not necessarily indicate an absence of affection. Quite the opposite. She laughs remembering one department potluck session on the importance of food-sharing in collective bonding.

A sudden idea. She starts from the couch. Slides in socks to the kitty cabinet and retrieves the treats, then slides back. Wordlessly, she scatters the whole bag of treats across the floor, to the boyfriend's shock.

At the sound of treats hitting wood, both cats come running.

They scavenge, distrustfully yet peacefully, it must be noted, in close vicinity to each other. And see? Ever-closer and closer, quite collaboratively, until every treat is gone.

They sniff around to make sure no treats remain.

Then they flee.

The boyfriend laughs.

The girlfriend is out front in gardening gloves. She is already sweating, hauling every one of her shiny new tools in a bucket from the dusty garage. She would be barefoot, enjoying grass between her toes, the simple luxury (no glass, no motor oil, no urine) if not for the presence of fire ants. She has an unopened bag of 5-5-5 at her feet but no clear plan for it as she squats over a bit of landscaping plastic embedded in the dry, grey, sandy dirt around the twin jasmine bushes at the end of the walkway cutting through their yard. She wonders why the plastic is there, what purpose it could possibly be serving aside from inhibiting the free circulation of water and beneficial critters and nutrients around the roots of potentially lovely, fragrant organisms. Which never bloomed, the uncle had complained to her, like he didn't know why, when it seemed common sense.

He'd offered the use of his wheelbarrow from the garage. As though she'd know the first thing to do with it. She has no budget for, nor any experience with gardening, only a simple human desire to meddle, and to save what is clearly dying. She knows nothing of soil quality, acidity, drainage, full sun versus partial shade, nor how to augment any of these. Nor how to avoid some further inadvertent harm to the plants and those who depend on them for their own survival, like bees and butterflies.

Everything about this is heavy. Fifteen years in the city, she'd never considered the difficulty of moving earth, only oneself. Only the feeling at the end of the day when her phone said she'd climbed twenty stories simply getting from place to place. Caring for herself alone was a burden. Conditions forced her to be selfish. In her mind then, the built city seemed to predate and overwhelm all living things, to have been already under construction at the dawn of time, and forevermore without end, fulfilling its destiny of intractability, unnavigability, humiliation, and frustration.

But what of how this ground itself predates us, she now considers. Its quality and purpose are different from the built environment. A different intractability. See how what grows out of this dirt resists being uprooted, holds in for its survival. This is a different power structure, a paradigm shift, a new value system that the girlfriend appreciates and relates to. Though it intimidates her since it asks more of her.

She had envisioned only the end of what she now considers is a long, slow process. She had imagined only the time once her plants were thriving, offering their flowers and fruits in gratitude. Never the lugging, dragging, sweating, and bearing of all they'll need across space, and over time. The cuts and scrapes and abrasions and burns, physical, emotional, and psychic, she'll incur in fighting for their lives, and sometimes losing. She remembers the sage words of an online guru, which she'd initially discarded as cruel: If you're not killing plants, you're not gardening.

She looks up at The Butter House and wipes her brow, leaving behind an adorable streak of dirt. The boyfriend is watching her through the window. He waves. She waves back and follows his gaze across the street to where their neighbor sits reading on a rocking chair on his porch. She's suddenly aware that she's on display for the whole block, and scans for Little Grey Cat, or any of the other multitude she's seen appearing and disappearing over the passing weeks, whenever she happens to step outside, and adding up in her imagination to a whole colony, similar in size to the one on her Brooklyn block, which had been there for generations, though unlike that one, this one was seeming to pass freely in and out of people's houses, as though enjoying some status of primacy and privilege among the neighborhood's inhabitants, human and nonhuman.

A certain fluffy Persian, skeletal beneath knotted fur, is likely the alpha. The girlfriend has surmised this from his slow, unhurried confidence, and the wide berth others give him. A stocky machismo Garfield is the second in line. Quite a bully, she thinks. Less so the tuxedo Sylvester cat she's seen with him, though she's still not a fan of his brand of masculinity: a bit aggressive, even desperate. Recently she saw him sniffing a plate of salmon skin she'd left on the front step especially for Little Grey Cat.

She's unearthing the last of the black, disintegrating plastic from beneath the jasmine when she hears, then turns to see, a tiger cat with a plaid collar coming through the jungle. He approaches her boldly, as though he knows her, or demands to know why he doesn't know her. Then he drags, aggressively, his entire length, head to tail, along her waist, and pauses with his rear on her elbow. They lock eyes.

He reverses himself, repeating the motion twice, then thrice: back, forth, back.

She greets him. Observes on his collar two rings: one bearing a yellow charm in the shape of a house, with an eight-hundred-number. The other one broken and empty, perhaps once bearing a name, a phone number, now gone.

Oh no. Maybe he's lost. Clearly he's someone's. She asks him where he lives. Scratching his head, she notices a bit of yellow around his eyes. She looks down the street one way, then the other. Sees no one on their porch anymore, hears no one whistling for him. He is purring madly as she rubs behind his ears and sweeps down his back, to where she sees the crook in his tail, where it had been broken.

When a cat slips out the door in a movie, it's an injection of fear into the narrative. A bad omen, sign of bad things to come. An indoor cat can't protect himself, his survival skills dulled with time and lack of use. He wants to be where he is comfy, protected, and fed. Outside he may lose his way, literal, figurative. He could be run over or eaten. Should you see him later in the film, it means there has been a miracle.

Their jolly mailman rounds the corner. He's pushing a blue cart on three wheels. His headphones partially compress a healthy afro, and his head bobs to muted heavy metal. He approaches their door and stuffs their letterbox full of mail for the previous tenant. The girlfriend smiles, waving as he passes back through the jasmine bushes, feeling mild and suburban. She notes his matching blue summer set, care of USPS, affording ventilation of calves and forearms. How happy he seems to be, sliding an additional letter into their next-door neighbor's box, already full, as though it hasn't been emptied in a long while. The curtains on either side of the front door are pulled.

She joins the boyfriend birdwatching, which he calls ornithological observation, at a nearby cemetery's muddy pond, teeming with alligator, turtle, carp, roseate spoonbill, flamingo, great blue- and tricolor heron, great white egret, and wood stork. They stalk marshy banks while anhinga submerge and resurface to warm their wings on headstones. Their spans spread in rows like garlands, leading toward the memorial rose gardens, in bloom. The girlfriend wonders whether roses grown in the garden are used in the cemetery's services, or whether these roses are some of the few nurtured for the sake of their living enjoyment.

Then the white ibis. Probing mud, foraging by feel for frogs, snails, snakes, and minnows. Brown speckled ibis are the adolescents, the boyfriend explains, lying out on soft grass with meats, cheese, sparkling water, strawberries, Rice Krispies treats, and his clipboard. Downy feathers harden and pale as they mature, and their beaks turn gray to orange. He doesn't remember them being here like this when he was a kid. Not in these numbers. He wonders whether in the last ten years or so, by his estimation, flocks have recovered from some precarity.

She admires what she perceives in him as a tendency to follow hope, foreign to her. This idea that the world can be safe despite people.

The afternoon melts. She slips into sleep, and he falls silent, observing. She wakes once to see him taking notes. Reaches across the blanket to rest her hand on his knee.

Lugging. Circling the pond's bottlebrush tree back toward The Butter House. Gloaming. Past the glittering mausoleum, back again past the drawers containing bodies or maybe ashes, the plaques, and stone steps to earthen landings, down again past the children's and veterans' fields. They turn down a path which opens onto a shady alcove, where tall Cyprus trees encircle a black obelisk, around which, chiseled into boulders, are smooth squares engraved with faces. Specifically, these are feline faces. No names. No dates.

But each face is unique. Each deceased.

And poised in the center of all of them, there before the girlfriend in the living flesh, as though enthroned among her forebears, blinking innocently, is Little Grey Cat.

The girlfriend is stunned, heart thumping. She reaches inside her bag for picnic chicken, the irony of its consumption while birdwatching only now dawning on her. She's never forgotten Little Grey Cat, has been surveilling each day for her on their street, hoping she's all right.

Then she stops. Peers over at the boyfriend. Who only moments before had been telling her of the plight of Australia: forced to cull three million stray cats from the country's streets. They had hunted to near-extinction certain species of songbirds. They don't even kill for food, he told her. They kill for fun.

But only if they're left outside, she said.

Now Little Grey Cat comes to The Butter House every morning. Green peepers pop up in the sunroom windows, shy eyes begging for breakfast. Fatigued after tripping the night fantastic, pleading and sad, it seems to the girlfriend, but there is potent gratitude in her meek expression when she sees the girlfriend coming. She purrs and curls her tail around the girlfriend's extended wrist, setting down her plate. The Butter House's hibiscus hedges are meant to shield the sunroom from gazes of passers-by. The girlfriend now uses them as leafy cover for her covert, unapproved feeding of this tiny hungry baby.

This is also so as not to attract others. Like Tiger Cat, though he's also never left the girlfriend's mind. Since their first meeting under the jasmine, she's noticed him sleeping on the porch next-door beneath the overstuffed, seemingly never-emptied mailbox. She's also seen some teenagers on that porch, looking rather alternative in greasy multi-colored hair, shredded jeans, and unseasonal flannel. In her imagination, she's ventured to ask them whether they know Tiger Cat or simply let him hang around, but her fear of seeming old, soft, uncool, and nosy has prevented her.

In fact, she's heard Tiger Cat caterwauling in her backyard. And those few times, admittedly, she has responded with food while pretending to take out the trash. But she fears making this a habit, setting precedents and expectations between Tiger

Cat and herself which she may someday be forced to disappoint.

She also fears attracting any judgy eyes of neighbors, like the youngish tattoo girl across the street, an obvious dog person. Or those of the boyfriend, who surely would disapprove of her caretaking the neighborhood's orphans. Who may not be as keen as she to adopt a third or fourth fur-child, however adorable or unofficial (for now). Especially given that she presently has no stream of income to refill her aquifers if she were to drain them on additional litter and food.

Plus, they have only lately achieved within their own home a delicate homeostasis among its various family members.

Still, one day she can't help it. She spies a grey question mark through the sunroom windows while her Round Guy is being a little piggy at the trough. He inhales his wet food, an adaptation to having to root through trash for his meals at a young age.

She steps between him and the bowl, signaling *take it easy.* She's over cleaning up his vomit, she reminds him.

She moves his bowl to the window, enticing him to follow, and he scampers right over. Where

Little Gray Cat is already waiting and watching him, curious.

Mewing sweetly.

Chunky Guy sees her and startles.

Lunges!

Yowling at the screen. Batting!

Surely from excitement, though, the girlfriend interprets. Simply a strong interest in making friends, not meant to be viewed as aggression. Not competition. Or territorialism.

Little Grey Cat rubs herself on the hibiscus, unbothered.

The boyfriend witnesses all of this.

Chuckles.

The girlfriend turns around to see him.

He shakes his head.

Finally there is rain. Gratitude on behalf of the small piece of supermarket ginger she's let sprout, then root in a humble corner of the yard. Mulching lovingly with leftover grounds to acidify the soil, having read that somewhere. Faithful clouds gathering midafternoon, cracking, lasting hours, torrential. The A/C suddenly stops working. The windows fog with an inability to see the flooding grass, or the cherished root, which may very well be drowning, and if so, then what would she do? She writes the boyfriend's initials on the windows and decorates them with kisses and hearts. Desperate, he discovers the HVAC is clogged with leaves while teetering upon two chairs held firmly in the girlfriend's fists. He reaches into the dark tunnel, warm, musty, and surely home to spiders. Drops an enormous clump of moldy leaves into a waiting salad bowl.

Sudden whooshing. Now chill air plus months of rain ahead promise no sweaty tangled sheets, nor hopefully any more dreams of mummification. Only cool steady pounding rhythm on the roof. Hot tea inside, watching road become river, reading novels. And worries of where Little Grey Cat hides to keep dry.

Indeed, where they all could be hiding. Those freely roaming unsupervised like children playing Manhunt. Climbing and sleeping upon any porch at random, multiplying beneath them, then their spawn scattering, and their kingdom growing. Little Grey Cat is but only one such wayward kitten.

Queen of Sheba is hiding. But needs to come out now because it's time for puma maintenance. It's probably best not to say as much aloud. She's always listening and isn't a fan of her daily cocktail of vitamins, appetite stimulant, anti-spasmodic, stomach enzyme, and laxative prescribed by her kitty doctor, to keep her *regular but not too regular*. She also does not much appreciate the biweekly subcutaneous saline drip given through a giant needle jabbed between her shoulder blades, but we don't want another unplanned sleepover at the vet now, do we? Not in her usual spot, nor the previous two favorites. Very sneaky. Where is that girl?

The girlfriend feels a stab with her sudden vision of the door not clicking while checking mail. Step-by-step replay. No. No. It did. It shut. And Miss Fancy Tail isn't a little escape artist like her brother. She's more likely to simply wander outside inadvertently, then get confused and forget why she came out here. Which is the reason the girlfriend ordered a new collar for her, with bespoke tag reading HELP ME I'M LOST.

Whereas her brother is already acclimated to the outdoors, and one could perhaps understand why he might feel nostalgic for the freedom and thrill of life on the block, or at least how he could confuse the familiarity of early programming for nostalgia. Missing the best of it, and by now the worst of it having faded from memory (unable to carry what no longer serves him). One year is an eternity in a lifespan brief as a cat's. Darting between cars, sleeping atop sewer vents, fighting with his claws out is now all distant memory. She's seen him sniffing about the front door. Even more lately, now that he has a friend outside who converses with him through the windows most mornings. Who also may be beckoning him to join her. Well, too bad.

Aha! Princess Puma is under the bed, wedged into a corner. Knowing full well what's up. Refusing to come out even though she's being asked very nicely. If the girlfriend were feeling cruel, she'd use the vacuum cleaner. On second thought, it isn't even an option, thanks to her very clever location protected by two walls at a right angle.

Seems it's time for a story.

The boyfriend is studying avian flight lines on a map atop the comforter. He pauses to greet her as she sits next to him. She's excited to show him the trick she's recently learned—or, shall she say, the magic she's conjured.

She opens a book and commences reading aloud. A curious title she found at the local library. She brought it home to commune more with the mingling fascination, horror, disgust, and self-recognition she found within its pages. It's a spark she's sought since finishing her formal training.

The book's author argues that domestic animals are little more than props on the sets of their owners' lives. Alive yet ossified, like sentient throw pillows, having been reduced to such a state by the removal of sex organs, rendering them permanent children. Then socially isolating them from others of their species. Further plying, training, and under-nourishing them with artificial food. In order to fulfil a selfish emotional, specifically human need. Individual to each so-called owner. Perhaps to satisfy themselves that a certain kind of love exists. Which cannot be negated by one who can't speak. Nor escape. Nor refuse. And is forced to accept the affection we insist on giving them. And forced to mirror it back to us as a tactic of their survival.

There's a rustle beneath the bed. A flourish of tail from the bed skirt.

The puma emerges.

Turns.

SARAH GERARD | 35

Makes eye contact. Meows.

The girlfriend continues reading aloud, a new tingle in her tummy, in anticipation of what's to come. Knowing the boyfriend is witnessing this, and feeling proud.

Without pausing in her reading, she offers the puma a direct invitation by patting the mattress beside her.

The puma springs.

Lands.

Announces herself, *brrrao!*

Her flirty tail flips to and 'fro. The girlfriend strokes the silky back of The Beautiful One, still reading.

The boyfriend has watched this all. Delighted to be presented with a calm and quite willing feline, ready to be prepped for the babysitter's arrival.

BLACK CAT —

- Keeps to herself but eventually will become curious about you
- Litterbox, food and water are set up in the back office, across from bathroom
- She is old and prefers to drink her food, mashed with water into loose slurry
- Sprinkle 1/8 teaspoon of Miralax onto it, for her to lick off
- Fresh water once a day in her glass jar, filled to the top, brimming
- Set water on a stack of books so she doesn't have to bend down to drink
- Set another glass on the windowsill
- She likes to gaze out at the birds and lap at the side of the glass
- Washcloth under the glass for spillage
- She likes being combed lightly, and it keeps her from getting hairballs or too hot
- She prefers the comb to the brush for this purpose
- She liked the laser pointer in her younger years, you could try it
- Good treats include a pinch of catnip left on the floor

- Keep the standing fan in the corner on low
- One white capsule (appetite stimulant) in case necessary—push into the back of her mouth and squirt her cheek with a syringe. This would require someone to hold her in a towel while you open her mouth. Hopefully this won't be necessary!

GREY STRIPES, WHITE PAWS —

- He will come right out and greet you
- Divide food in two bowls: half and half (he eats too fast)
- Give him the first bowl and then the second fifteen/twenty minutes later
- Wait for a few minutes and watch him eat, in case he throws up
- Don't let him run for half an hour after he eats
- Fresh water in his glass jar, filled all the way to the top, brimming
- Maybe set a few of glasses around the room where he'll happen upon them
- He is very friendly, likes to play, and will chase the balls from the metal bowl
- Favorites are sparkly pom-poms and plastic springs, anything dangly, twinkly
- He likes being chased and might chase you and play tag
- He will brush himself if you hold the brush firmly
- He is very curious—too curious!
- Very mischievous and often knows better
- He will stick his whole head in the catnip jar

The uncle's husband is recounting for them, over roast hen, their own family-blending saga. The husband's cat is his King and would not concede his throne. Couldn't tolerate a third man in the house. They have a good hearty laugh over a story of welcome-home Tootsie Rolls in the uncle's shoes. Everyone laughs except the uncle, who pouts and demands an end to the cattitude. He reminds his husband that Mister Thing in his fancy tuxedo was a nibbler—nay, a biter, with pressure ranging from affection to aggression, leaving literal scars on ankles. Plus, he has an agitated general demeanor and sour countenance, and would benefit from a prescription to Prozac. Thrashes his crooked tail, gnashes his crooked teeth. Has no friends in the neighboring yards, as far as the uncle can tell. And he refuses to be antagonized by a non-rent-paying, non-human transient.

The uncle's husband guffaws. Labels this a pure projection. The cat after all was here first, was he not? And is very old and has been battered by a lifetime of indoor/outdoor access. His general bad mood is unable to be helped. It isn't personal.

The uncle takes things too personally, the boyfriend and girlfriend agree. It isn't about him. They share, tentatively, some of their own early journey toward familyhood. The ongoing unrest, constant scuffles and mediation, and the monthly cost of a Feliway Plug-In subscription, and how the cloying scent of feline pleasure pheromones concentrated for spray-bottle application clings to their clothes.

Yet they reaffirm that the cats truly love The Butter House, as do they both themselves. They're feeling more at home in it all the time, the girlfriend continues. She attributes their contentment to the perching birds, bunnies, and ample foliage and sunlight of the subtropics. They feel so rested and renewed, inspired, reinvigorated, reanimated, after nearly succumbing to urban malaise. And suffering her years of school, her Little Guy burning the midnight oil with her. Exhaustion, truly. Animals have basic needs, like sleep and sun and socialization and recreation and exercise.

Speaking of which. Lately, the garden has been a source of solace for her. Though yes, tiring, but the quality of which was different from the aforementioned exhaustion—perhaps, it occurs to her now, because it feels purposeful. She can behold and even consume, immediately or continuously over time, the thankful fruits of her labor. Smell and touch them. Know they are good. See and understand and care for them without dissecting and labeling and pathologizing their inner workings. In fact, it's wonderful to observe how time and worldly cares seem to slip away while she's weeding around the tomato plants, and verbal thought disappears from her mind, revealing a hidden grammar beneath consciousness, older than any language. She's found that in its presence she feels smaller, yet more at peace with her cosmic insignificance. Less human, more being.

She tells them about conversing with Tiger Cat, who likes to visit from next door. His eyes are growing red and inflamed, and crusty yellow has built up around the lids, as though no one has wiped them let alone treated them with drops. She leaves food for him in the back, out of sight of other cats who surely see more clearly than he does, and who therefore have an advantage competing for resources. He's longhaired yet angular, malnourished, with brown and black stripes. His tail is losing fur. Do they know him?

A sad case, yes, says the uncle. He recognizes the description. Tiger Cat belongs next-door. Their neighbor's husband passed away in conjunction with, but not directly due to the last hurricane (heart attack, crowded ER), leaving two teenagers and her a widow. The kids are more or less orphans due to their mother's consequent drinking. They rove all hours, like Tiger Cat. The girlfriend did finally attempt to offer a simple hello to them while out walking, but they sneered at her.

Still, Tiger Cat's caterwauling pains her. While she's making French toast, he yowls as though he were there in the kitchen with her, begging for food. And instead of feeding him, someone were repeatedly stepping on his tail. The sound reverberates in her skull day and night. Sinks inside her like a precious stone in a dark pond.

Ah! Look who it is now, come to join them, says the uncle. A visitor. Your Royal Highness, Madame Hot Wings gracing them with her presence. The Dowager Empress, the boyfriend's uncle's other life mate. She is less of an issue, pro-socially speaking, than his husband's bloodthirsty Heel Hunter. Physically? Well, a different story. She takes supplements. Glucosamine chondrointin for arthritis, Renal K for the kidneys. Gabapentin, a mood stabilizer, which may or may not be causing a slight wobble in her step, but if they don't dose her then she hides in the fireplace when there's company. She's terrified of all people and sudden noises and movements. Amlodypine they give her for what, they can't recall, but they trust their vet implicitly—

with their own lives, if necessary. She's an actual living saint who does world-class feline research, which is grossly underfunded compared to canine research. She's taken their calls in the middle of the night. She was even at their wedding. She sources them the saline they use for weekly subcutaneous hydrations at wholesale. The needles, they have to buy on eBay.

Look at her. Big Foot shambles across the plush rug, each step a combined effort of muscle, bone, breath, and blood, fighting against gravity. The uncle gazes upon her affectionately. His Blueberry Muffin. Cupcake. Coloration the same as the girlfriend's own guy: white socks shorter but feet longer, heels lower to the ground. She is thin and unsteady in grey furs, draped on a brittle frame, swaying with her humpty gait. She used to chase the dangly toy for hours. Now look at her.

She stops before her feeding station. Inspects it. An absolute flower, looking back up at her audience with her daisy face. Waiting for someone to rise to the occasion. The uncle's husband stands to address her. Your Highness. He proceeds to the pantry and extracts a packet of FortiFlora probiotic. He tears it open and shakes it over her food.

She *ma-ows* and lopes over. Turns toward him

back to her bowl, crossing her ankles, nearly tripping on herself.

They learn that she's recently had an upper respiratory infection, with some lingering congestion. Therefore she can't always smell or taste what is edible, or whether there is food to be enjoyed. Once she knows it's there, though, her appetite is bottomless. That meat powder activates. It's downright Pavlovian. A total drug.

She falls on it, snorfling.

What a snugglebug.

They stay in the aquarium room. The uncle and his husband have a total of eighty fish in eight tanks of various sizes and shapes, some tall and narrow, freestanding, some long and laid atop a dresser or table. A countertop nightlight in the adjoining bathroom illuminates vases and dishes with rosy betta, crab and seashell soaps, and seahorse towel hooks. The comforter is bedecked in parakeets, banded snakes, lemurs, and tigers to match rattan curtains and windows overlooking swamp. Bamboo wallpaper. Carved teak bedposts. A shellacked alligator's head atop a pirate's treasure chest. Which the girlfriend won't open, she promises, no matter how curious she is about what may be inside. Like funny sex toys. Or weird taxidermy. Or a hundred VHS copies of *Kazaam*, never opened. It's probably linens, says the boyfriend. But how is he so certain? There is only one way to know.

The tanks hum. She tours them. They're stocked with tropical freshwater breeds. Electric yellow line cleaners and burgundy urchins and electric flame scallops and aquamarine triggers and leopards and orange oscillaris clowns and orchid dottybacks and maroon snowflakes and coral banded shrimp and chocolate chip starfish and purple firefish and half black angelfish and green neon tetras and harlequin rasboras and orange swordfish and rainbow sharks and oscars and firemouth cichlids and black ghost knightfish and suckermouth catfish, as though naming them can bring us any closer to what they are, or make their lives mean more.

The tanks are dark in the morning. The fish still. Madame Dowager sits gazing into a softly humming world beyond her reach. Mockingbirds trill outside.

Back at The Butter House, an orange cat with one eye waits on the stoop. The girlfriend has seen him from a distance, unsure whether the missing eye was an illusion. For the eye to be missing in the way that it is, she figures, it must have been surgically removed. So someone is keeping or was keeping an eye on him (she cringes at her joke). There's no tab on his ear to indicate he's a neutered stray. Yet there is no collar, either. And he's tiny, beyond slim. And seeking nourishment.

She ducks inside, into the kitty cabinet. Filling a bowl, she listens for the sound of Tiger Cat. Hears nothing. Wonders who else may be listening for him.

She leaves a bowl on the back step, then rounds their yard to the front. The orange cat is still there, waiting with one eye closed forever. She slides a bowl of kibble behind the lemongrass she planted to keep away mosquitoes, and reenters the house through the front. She sits down at the kitchen table.

Dear neighbors,

I've been told the brown tabby with the plaid collar belongs to you. He's very sweet. He often comes into our yard, and I occasionally feed him. I've noticed him getting skinnier in recent months. This is concerning, as the weather will change someday, and he'll need extra fat to keep warm. I've also noticed that the infections in his eyes are not going away. Here's some money to help you take him to the vet.

Yours truly,

Fellow animal lover